A NOTE TO PARENTS

When your children are ready to "step into reading," giving them the right books—and lots of them—is as crucial as giving them the right food to eat. **Step into Reading Books** present exciting stories and information reinforced with lively, colorful illustrations that make learning to read fun, satisfying, and worthwhile. They are priced so that acquiring an entire library of them is affordable. And they are beginning readers with an important difference—they're written on four levels.

Step 1 Books, with their very large type and extremely simple vocabulary, have been created for the very youngest readers. **Step 2 Books** are both longer and slightly more difficult. **Step 3 Books,** written to mid-second-grade reading levels, are for the child who has acquired even greater reading skills. **Step 4 Books** offer exciting nonfiction for the increasingly proficient reader.

Children develop at different ages. **Step into Reading Books,** with their four levels of reading, are designed to help children become good—and interested—readers *faster*. The grade levels assigned to the four steps—preschool through grade 1 for Step 1, grades 1 through 3 for Step 2, grades 2 and 3 for Step 3, and grades 2 through 4 for Step 4—are intended only as guides. Some children move through all four steps very rapidly; others climb the steps over a period of several years. These books will help your child "step into reading" in style!

To Kathy

Photo credits: pp. 6, 7, 36, 41, 44, Copyright © 1976 by Lee Boltin; pp. 22–23, 34–35, 42–43, Photography by Egyptian Expedition, The Metropolitan Museum of Art; p. 26, Griffith Institute, Ashmolean Museum, Oxford.

Library of Congress Cataloging-in-Publication Data:
Donnelly, Judy.
   Tut's mummy: lost...and found. (Step into reading. A Step 3 book) SUMMARY: Describes the burial of the pharaoh Tutankhamen and the discovery of his long-lost tomb by archaeologists more than 3,000 years later.
1. Tutankhamen, King of Egypt—Tomb—Juvenile literature.   2. Egypt—Antiquities—Juvenile literature.
3. Excavations (Archaeology)—Egypt—Juvenile literature. [1. Tutankhamen, King of Egypt—Tomb.   2. Egypt—Antiquities.   3. Excavations (Archaeology)—Egypt] I. Watling, James, ill. II. Title. III. Series: Step into reading. Step 3 book. DT87.5.D66   1988   932'.01'0924   87-20790   ISBN: 0-394-89189-9 (pbk.);
0-394-99189-3 (lib. bdg.)

Manufactured in the United States of America   4 5 6 7 8 9 0

Step into Reading

TUT'S MUMMY

LOST...AND FOUND

By Judy Donnelly

Illustrated by James Watling

A Step 3 Book

Random House 🏠 New York

1
The King Is Dead

"Tutankhamen is dead! The boy king is dead!" The news travels through Egypt. King Tutankhamen (too-tonk-AH-men) was only eighteen years old. His wife and family are very sad to lose him. But the Egyptians are glad for their king.

They believe his spirit will travel to a wonderful place—the Land of the Dead.

There the king will do all the things he loved to do when he was alive. He will feast and play games. He will go hunting and fishing. His spirit will be happy forever.

Tutankhamen will need many things in the Land of the Dead. He will need food and furniture and clothing. He will need games and jewelry. All these things must be buried with him.

A golden necklace that belonged to the king

A gameboard buried with the king

Most of all, the king will need his body. The Egyptians believe a spirit cannot live on without its body. So dead bodies are dried out to last forever. They are turned into mummies.

Priests come to the palace. They say prayers for the king. Then they dry out the king's body. They use a special kind of salt called natron. It takes many days. The mummy is wrapped in yards of fine cloth. More than one hundred jewels and charms are tucked in the folds. The charms will keep evil spirits away from the king.

It takes seventy days to make a mummy. But finally the mummy is ready.

Now it is time for the funeral. It is time for the king's spirit to travel to the Land of the Dead.

Tutankhamen's mummy must be kept in a very safe place. At one time Egyptian kings were buried in giant pyramids. But

robbers broke into all of them. They
stole the treasure. So Tutankhamen will
be buried in a secret underground tomb.

The king's funeral begins. A long
parade walks slowly to the Nile River.
The king's gold coffin shines in the sun.

The young queen walks nearby.
She prays aloud.

The Egyptians believe some gods take the shape of animals. So there are priests in leopard skins and animal masks. They chant and sing. One priest wears the mask of a dog. He is supposed to be Anubis, the god of mummies.

Women cry and tear at their clothing. They are showing how sad they are to lose their king.

Behind them come hundreds of servants. They carry the king's treasure. They carry chests of clothes and jewels. They bring weapons and chariots. They carry baskets of flowers and food and wine.

The servants also bring hundreds of tiny statues. These statues are supposed to turn into magic servants in the Land of the Dead. There they will serve the king.

Beautiful boats carry the people and the treasure across the river. They are going to a rocky, deserted valley.

The king's coffin is put onto a kind of sled. It is pulled up a rocky path.

The people follow behind. It is hot and dusty. They walk for miles. Finally they reach the secret entrance to the valley. Here is the royal graveyard. Priests guard it day and night.

An opening has been cut into the rocky ground. A fire burns beside it. This is Tutankhamen's secret tomb.

The priests pray. They touch the mouth, eyes, and ears on the mummy. Now the king's spirit can speak and see and hear.

The mummy is put in the coffin and carried inside the tomb. With it goes all the king's treasure.

A great funeral feast begins. There is music and dancing. There is food and wine.

At last the feast is over. The entrance to the tomb is filled up with stones. Now the tomb is hidden. Perhaps this will keep robbers away.

Everyone goes back across the river. They are happy now. The king is on his way to a new life.

2
The Lost King

More than three thousand years go by. The giant pyramids still stand in the desert. But Egypt's great days are long gone.

Rulers from other lands have taken over. The old beliefs are gone. No more kings are buried with treasure. No more mummies are made. Tutankhamen's name is forgotten. So is his tomb.

Then, in the 1800s, something happens. People become interested in ancient times. Travelers pour into Egypt. They visit the temples and pyramids. They all try to bring something back—pottery, beads, statues, even mummies!

Some of the visitors are <u>archaeologists</u> (ar-kee-AHL-o-jists). They are scientists who dig in the earth to find clues to the past. They travel far from the Nile. They go into the desert. They dig in the sand.

They uncover forgotten temples. They find beautiful wall paintings and strange statues of animals and gods.

The archaeologists find mummies—
thousands of them. There are mummies of
men, women, and children. There are
even animal mummies. Mummy cats.
Mummy bulls. Mummy crocodiles. Even
mummy insects!

Every archaeologist dreams of finding the tomb of a king. A tomb that has never been robbed.

Scientists begin to dig in a lonely valley. It is called the Valley of the Kings.

One man uncovers a hidden tomb. It belongs to a famous king. Soon dozens of other tombs are discovered.

But the tombs are all empty. Robbers looted them long, long ago.

By 1900, most people have given up on the valley. Every inch has been dug up, they say. No other tombs are there.

But one English archaeologist does not agree. His name is Howard Carter. He thinks one king is still buried in the valley. Tutankhamen.

3
The Search

Other scientists think Howard Carter is foolish. The valley is empty. They are sure of it.

But Howard is stubborn. He first came to Egypt when he was only seventeen years old. For years he worked in the valley. He knows it very well. He is sure Tutankhamen's tomb is there. And he is going to find it.

Some clues have been found—a cup, a few jars, some thin sheets of gold. And all of them bear the name Tutankhamen.

But all the clues were found near the empty tomb of another king. Too near, everyone says. The Egyptians wouldn't put two tombs so close together. Would they?

Lord Carnarvon

Howard does not listen to anybody. And he is lucky. He meets a rich Englishman who believes in him. The man's name is Lord Carnarvon. He gives Howard the money he needs to start his search.

Howard hires fifty men. Then he sets out for the valley.

It is a terrible place. There are no
trees or grass. Just rocky cliffs and sand.
It is burning hot, dry and dusty. The rocks
give no shade. But they are good hiding
places for snakes and insects.

Howard doesn't mind. He and his men
start to work. It is hard and slow. The men
fill baskets with stones and sand. They
carry them off and empty them. Then they
come back for more.

At last they hit something. But it is not a king's tomb. They find some old stone huts. Howard is very disappointed. He moves to a different part of the valley.

He digs there for five long years. What does he find? Nothing.

Finally Lord Carnarvon has had enough. He wants to give up. Not Howard. He begs for one more try.

He remembers those stone huts. He wants to dig under them. It is one place no one has ever tried.

Lord Carnarvon agrees. But this is Howard's last chance.

Howard buys a golden canary for good luck. And in November 1922, he and his men start digging again.

On the third day Howard and his men find a step! It is cut right into the rock. They uncover another and another. They have found a whole stairway! And it leads to a secret door.

Howard is burning with excitement. What is behind that door? But he cannot forget Lord Carnarvon. Lord Carnarvon is far away in England. He will want to be there too.

Howard sends his friend the thrilling news.

Lord Carnarvon sets out right away. But there aren't many airplanes in 1922. He has to come by ship, train, another ship, another train, and last, by donkey. It takes two whole weeks!

Finally the two men stand before the secret door. Howard sees some writing he has not noticed before. There is a name: TUTANKHAMEN!

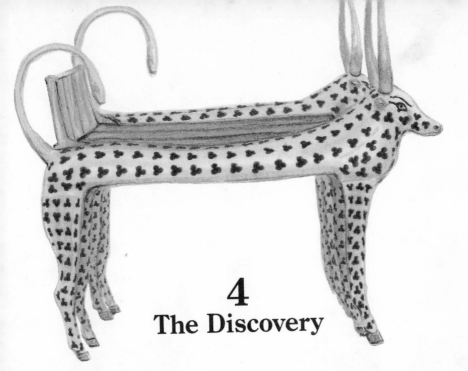

4
The Discovery

Carefully Howard makes a hole in the door. He holds a candle to the opening. Lord Carnarvon is right behind him. "Do you see anything?" he asks.

Howard cannot speak. Then he chokes out some words. "Yes," he says. "Wonderful things!"

There are golden chariots, jeweled chests, couches in the shapes of animals. There are vases and statues. Everything glitters with gold!

The first room of treasure that Howard found

Tutankhamen's throne

Soon Howard is standing inside the tomb.

He is almost afraid. The air smells sweet from ancient funeral flowers. Time seems to melt away. He feels as if the king were buried only moments ago.

He sees two statues of the king, big as life. He sees Tutankhamen's golden throne. Excitement takes over. Treasure is all around him. It is piled to the ceiling. And there are doors to still more rooms! One of them is sealed shut. Howard is sure the king's mummy is somewhere behind it, waiting.

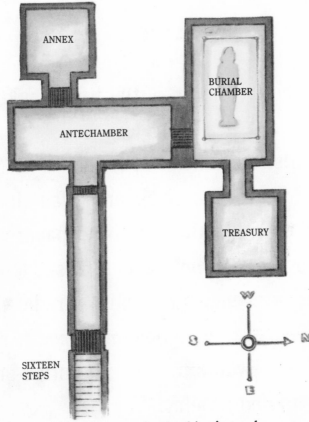

All the rooms in the king's tomb

5
The King Is Found

The discovery of the tomb makes headlines all over the world. It is the greatest treasure ever found.

Howard Carter becomes famous. And so does Tutankhamen. Newspapers call him King Tut for short. And suddenly his name is everywhere—on the radio, in the movies, even in songs and jokes. And everyone wants to wear Egyptian-style clothes and jewelry.

Howard wants to open the sealed door right away. But first hundreds of treasures must be cleared out. And they must be moved very, very carefully. Howard has learned this the hard way. Once he touched a beaded necklace. The thread turned to dust. Beads scattered everywhere. Howard had to pick up each one with a tweezer. All 371 beads!

It takes months to clear the tomb. But finally Howard is ready to find the king's mummy.

Very carefully he opens the sealed door. At first he sees only a wall of gold! It is a huge golden cabinet. Inside the cabinet is a great stone box. And in the box are THREE beautiful coffins. Each coffin is nested tight inside the other. The picture below shows how it looked.

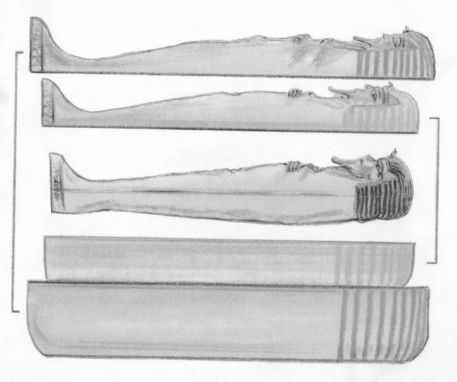

The last coffin is made of solid gold.
More than two hundred pounds of it.

Slowly Howard takes out the golden nails. It is a special moment. Once Tutankhamen was just a name to him. Now he has seen the king's face on

Howard at work on the third coffin

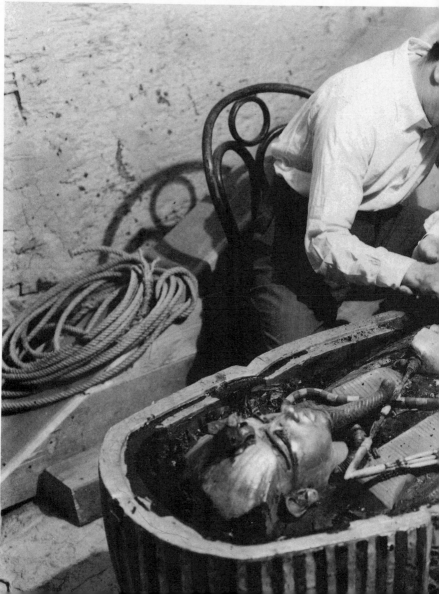

statues and carvings. He has touched the king's dearest belongings. His robes and sandals. His games. The chair he sat on as a small child.

Howard raises the golden lid. There
is the mummy of the king. It wears a
beautiful gold mask. Beneath the mask,
the mummy is covered with cloth. Gently
Howard takes the cloth away. He sees the
face of the dead king for the first time. It
is the face of a young man. He looks calm
and peaceful.

It is hard for Howard to understand that even now people fear the king's mummy. They believe it has magic powers.

The story starts because Lord Carnarvon dies not long after going into the tomb. He dies from a bad insect bite. But newspapers say it is because of the mummy's curse. They say Tut is mad that his tomb has been opened. And now he has gotten back at Lord Carnarvon.

Howard does not believe mummies have magic powers. After all, he is the one who opened the tomb. Not Lord Carnarvon. And Howard is fine. In fact, he lives for many years.

Howard sends Tut's treasures to a museum. He wants scientists to study them. He wants millions of people to enjoy them.

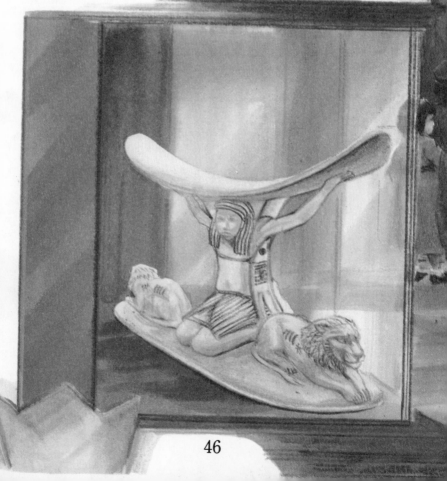

But he feels there is only one place for King Tut's mummy. King Tut will stay where he has rested for 3,300 years. He will stay in his royal tomb.

Most people feel that no one will ever find another wonderful royal tomb in Egypt. Some do not agree. They are in the Valley of the Kings today, searching.

And at least one royal tomb has never been found. The tomb of King Tut's father.